NINA CREWS

A High, Low, Near, Far, Loud, Quiet Story

Greenwillow Books, New York

For the McGovern-Johnsons

and the McGovern-Edisons

Special thanks to Ivy and Nate Johnson
and their mother, Justine McGovern,
for bringing this book to life

The full-color photographs were printed from
35-mm negatives. The text type is Swiss 721.

Printed in Hong Kong by
South China Printing Company (1988) Ltd.

First Edition 1 2 3 4 5 6 7 8 9 10

Library of Congress Cataloging-in-Publication Data

Crews, Nina.
A high, low, near, far, loud, quiet story / by Nina Crews.
      p.   cm.
Summary: Labeled photographs present opposites
such as fast and slow, large and small, and rough
and smooth.
ISBN 0-688-16794-2 (trade).
ISBN 0-688-16795-0 (lib. bdg.)
1. English language—Synonyms and antonyms—
Juvenile literature.   [1. English language—
Synonyms and antonyms.]
I. Title.   PE1591.C72   1999   428.1—dc21
98-33273   CIP   AC

DAY

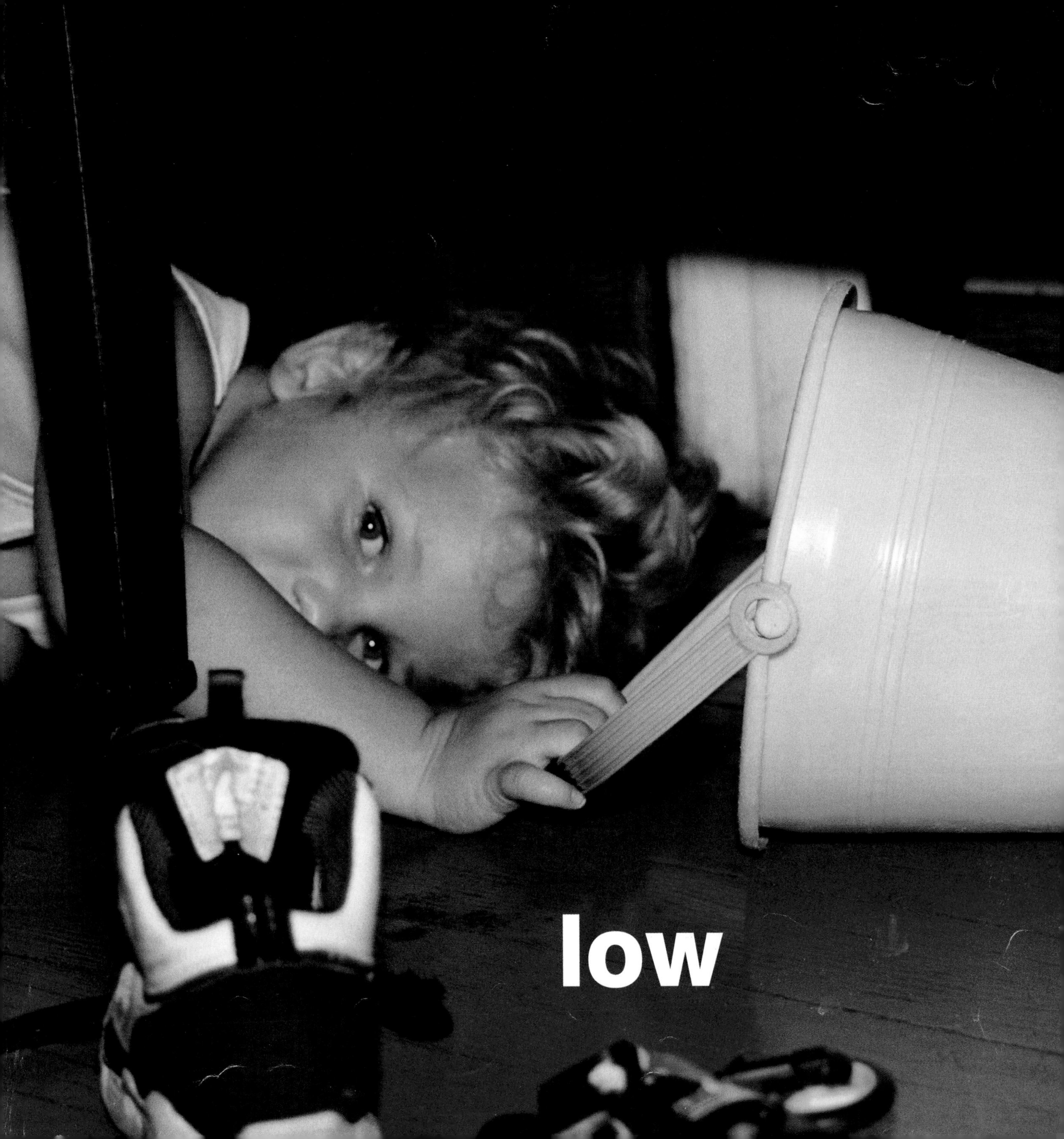

low

fast

slow

large

small

rough

smooth

empty

full

wide

narrow

wet

dry

outside

inside

loud

quiet

near

NIGHT